*Tales for a Winter's Eve*

*Wendy Watson*

# TALES FOR A WINTER'S EVE

*A Sunburst Book*

*Farrar, Straus and Giroux*

FOR LEWIS

Library of Congress catalog card number: 87–13467
Published in Canada by HarperCollins*CanadaLtd*
Printed and bound in the United States of America
First edition, 1988
Sunburst edition, 1991

# Contents

# DUSK

"YAHOO!" FREDDIE Fox shot over the crest of the hill, his skis kicking up a spray of snow behind him. Ahead, the trail swooped down through clumps of juniper and disappeared from view.

Freddie crouched lower as he swerved around the bushes. Just then, his skis hit a branch on the path and he was airborne, flipping and spinning in a cloud of snow.

"Oof!" Freddie landed with a thud. Carefully he brushed the snow from his eyes. He wiggled his toes. One paw hurt. Then he saw that his leather bindings had ripped loose from his skis.

"Oh no!" yipped Freddie. "Now I'll have to walk all the

way home." He struggled to get up, wincing as he put his weight on his twisted paw. Behind him, deep blue shadows crept down the mountain. Far below, he saw pinpricks of candlelight flickering up in the windows along Vinegar Lane.

Suddenly an owl hooted. Freddie shivered, and his heart beat faster. Quickly he slung his skis over his shoulder and began to limp downhill, toward food and warmth.

Deep in the Fox burrow, supper was almost ready. Mama Fox pulled tins of muffins from the oven. George, Henry, and Ella, Freddie's older brothers and sister, set the table. Grammer sat knitting by the fire, while Papa and Granky carried in armloads of wood. Even Nellie Mouse and Bert Blue Jay were there, gossiping in a corner.

"I wonder where Freddie is," said Ella.

"He thought he'd be home before dark," Mama said, looking out the window. As she turned back to the oven, Freddie came into the warm room.

"Thank goodness you're home at last," cried Mama, hugging Freddie. "But you're limping! And your skis are broken."

Freddie's mouth began to tremble.

"Now, now," said Granky, putting his arm around Freddie. "Tell us what happened."

Everyone crowded around to hear Freddie's story. By the time he had finished, his paw hurt so much that he started to cry.

"Come," said Mama. "Let me rub your paw with some of my herbal salve. That will make it better."

"I'll tell you a tale to help you forget the ache," said Grammer.

"I'll mend your skis after supper," said Papa. "They'll be good as new."

So Mama and Nellie Mouse bandaged Freddie's paw, and Bert Blue Jay helped settle him next to Papa's chair. Then everyone found a seat around the long wooden table.

Freddie took a crusty muffin and passed the basket on to Grammer, but he couldn't eat. His paw throbbed.

"Grammer," he whispered, "what about your tale?"

"Ah yes," said Grammer. She took a bite of muffin. "Here's a tale," she said with her mouth full, "a tale about muffins." She wiped her whiskers.

# GRAMMER'S TALE

"ONE MORNING," Grammer began, "Weedie Woodchuck, way down at the end of Vinegar Lane, got her six children up early.

" 'Sally, Sarah, Samuel, Simon, Samantha, Stefanie,' Weedie called. 'Mr. Raccoon, the governor, is coming to dinner, and you must help clean house.'

" 'Hooray! The governor!' the children cried. They'd never had Mr. Raccoon visit before.

"But then they thought of the housework, and their faces fell. So Weedie promised that if they got their chores done, she'd bake a triple batch of her famous lighter-than-air muffins for dinner, and they could each have as many as they wanted.

" 'That's fair,' the children agreed, and they set to work. They scrubbed and swept and dusted all day, and dreamed about their reward.

"When the governor arrived, everyone sat down at the dinner table. Weedie passed the muffin basket around, and Sally, Sarah, Samuel, Simon, Samantha, and Stefanie each took one. But Mr. Raccoon took five! and began to gobble them down. The Woodchuck children stared. Then Sally spoke up.

" 'This corn bread is mighty good,' she said. 'Won't you have some?'

" 'No, thank you,' Mr. Raccoon replied. 'These muffins will do me just fine.' And he took five more.

"Well—Weedie's children tried to eat faster, but they were no match for Mr. Raccoon. Each time they had one muffin, he had four or five. The children got more and more perturbed, watching him, and when Mr. Raccoon helped himself to the last three muffins, little Stefanie began to cry.

" 'A bawling woodchuck comes to no good,' said the governor, with a burp, and he started to push back his chair. Weedie was the first to see his danger.

" 'Keep your knees under the table!' she hollered. 'Those muffins are lighter than air!'

"But Mr. Raccoon was already afloat. He bobbed out of his chair, lost hold of the tablecloth, and went surging, willy-nilly, up toward the rafters. Samuel opened the door just then to get some wood, and the rush of hot air pulled the governor right outside. He started skyward, and would have kept straight on to the moon, I suppose, except that his suspenders got caught on a branch of that pear tree in Weedie's front yard.

" 'Leave him till it wears off,' said the children.

"But Weedie was afraid Mr. Raccoon would freeze to death, out in that cold. Then it started to snow, a heavy sticky snow, and that added just enough weight to bring him down to where Weedie could get a rope around his leg. She had to do it by herself, too—the children wouldn't help a bit. She wrestled Mr. Raccoon into the spare room and tied him up to the bedpost so there wouldn't be another mishap.

"In the middle of the night, the Woodchuck family woke up to a big loud thud. That was the governor, coming down hard. The next morning, he left without breakfast, and he never could look the Woodchuck children in the eyes again.

"That evening, Weedie baked another triple batch of muffins, so Sally, Sarah, Samuel, Simon, Samantha, and Stefanie finally did get their reward."

Grammer leaned over to kiss Freddie. "And that's my tale about muffins."

"Time now for dessert," said Mama. "Rose-hip pudding. Freddie—here, I'll serve you first."

As Freddie passed his bowl, two tears rolled down his cheeks.

"Why, Freddie, what's the matter?" asked Papa.

"Mama's salve isn't working yet," sobbed Freddie. "And I'm too hot."

"Freddie needs another tale," said his brother George.

Then Bert Blue Jay spoke up.

"You're too hot, Freddie? Come over here where it's cooler. I'll tell you a tale about someone who was even hotter than you are."

Freddie moved over next to Bert and took a big bite of pudding as the story began.

# BERT BLUE JAY'S TALE

"I WAS IN Mr. Twing's store late one afternoon," Bert said, "watching a game of checkers by the stove, and getting warmed up a bit before I went home. As I turned around to toast the other side, the bell on the door clanged, and in walked that rascal, Smart the Weasel.

" 'What's the weather?' someone called out.

" 'Like a miser's heart, and growing colder,' said Smart. He went to the counter, and I turned my attention back to the game.

"By and by, I noticed that Smart was still at the counter, and Mr. Twing was running from one end of the store to the other, waiting on him. First Twing brought out a bag of nails, then an eggbeater and a pair of rubber boots. Next I saw a teapot added to the pile, and a wrench, and a pound of butter.

"When I looked again, Twing was returning with another armful of goods. But before he could put them down, Smart began to button up his coat.

" 'Guess I won't buy anything, after all,' Smart said.

"Twing was fit to be tied. He started to gather the things back up, when he got a sharp look on his face. He bustled out from behind the counter and grabbed Smart's sleeve.

" 'Now, now, can't be going out into that cold so soon,' Mr. Twing cried, and he drew Smart up to the stove in such a friendly fashion that we all had to stare.

" 'No, got to be leaving,' Smart mumbled, trying to pull away.

"Twing pushed him down into a chair. 'Ha, ha,' he laughed. 'Sit and stay awhile.' He reached for Smart's scarf and hat.

" 'No!' Smart bellowed, so loud we all jumped, and he grabbed on to his hat with both paws. 'I caught a chill and have to stay warm!'

" 'Well, then,' said Mr. Twing, 'let's heat your innards with some ginger nog,' and he busied himself with a pan.

"By this time, Smart couldn't have left without looking foolish, so he sat and drank a steaming mug of Mr. Twing's

ginger nog. The stove was mighty hot, too, and pretty soon I saw the sweat starting to trickle down Smart's forehead.

" 'Must've warmed up a bit by now,' said Twing. 'Let me hang up your things.'

" 'No, thanks!' Smart cried as he jerked back. 'I'm still a mite cold.' Now the sweat was coming down in rivers from under his hat, and it flew through the air in globs as he moved.

" 'Tarnation,' one of the fellows muttered. 'That isn't sweat—that must be his brains melting away.'

"Just at that moment, Twing finally got hold of Smart's hat and snatched it off his head.

" 'There!' Twing hollered. 'Now you can see why Smart's in such a sweat!'

"We all stared, and our mouths dropped open. Sitting on Smart's head were the remains of that fine pound of butter I'd seen earlier on the counter, melting into his fur, and dribbling down on all sides.

"Well, we all burst out laughing, even Mr. Twing, and we laughed till we cried. Smart slunk out of there with his tail between his legs, and it was a long time before he showed his face in the village again."

Bert Blue Jay chuckled. "So you see, Freddie, Smart's seat was even hotter than yours."

Sparks snapped as Granky threw a fresh log on the fire. Papa reached for Freddie's broken skis.

"Are you feeling better now?" he asked.

"Yes," said Freddie. "But I'm bored. It's hard to sit still." He leaned closer to Papa. "Another tale would help," he murmured.

Nellie Mouse's nose twitched. "Bored, are you?" she asked. "And wanting another tale? Perhaps I can oblige." She threaded a needle with a strand of yarn.

# NELLIE MOUSE'S TALE

"ONE YEAR," Nellie began, "my big cousins from the city came to visit for the holidays. But when they got here, things were too quiet for them. Day after day they told us how bored they were. I guess that was why they spent so much time bossing me around.

"Then one morning a couple of strangers came down Vinegar Lane and plastered up a sign at Twing's store. My cousins rushed me over to see what was happening.

"THE INCREDIBLE GROLLYBASH, they read. THE MOST FEROCIOUS MONSTER EVER SEEN IN THESE PARTS. ADMISSION 5 CENTS. TOWN HALL, 7 P.M. SHARP.

"Well, that was what my cousins needed. 'You'll come with us, Nellie,' they said, and after supper we set out. When we got to the Town Hall, one of the strangers took our nickels at the door.

" 'Hurry up, Nellie,' my cousins hissed. Dragging me along by the arms, they wriggled their way through the crowd toward the front of the room. There were some fringed curtains strung up on wires to make a stage, and we squeezed onto the floor between the curtains and the first row of seats.

"Right at seven o'clock, the same stranger came out from behind the curtains.

" 'Ladies and gentlemen!' he began.

"As the crowd quieted down, I could hear snorting and the clanking of chains from backstage. I was so excited that I began to tie my bootlaces in knots.

"The stranger continued. 'Tonight you will see one of the earth's most savage—'

" 'Tom!' came a cry from backstage. 'Give me a hand!'

"With a yelp, the stranger sprang behind the curtains. There were fierce growls amid the clankings and snorts. I tied more and more knots, as fast as I could.

" 'Hold him!' cried one voice from backstage.

" 'He's getting away!' barked the other.

"Suddenly the stranger burst back through the curtains.

" 'Ladies and gentlemen,' he bawled. 'The Grollybash has broken his chains! *Run for your lives!*'

"Instantly the audience leaped to its feet and began a mad rush for the door. My cousins scrambled up.

" 'Come on, Nellie!' they hissed. They tried to pull me after them, but something had hold of my foot and wouldn't let go.

" 'I can't!' I gasped. My cousins looked back.

" 'She's tied herself to the curtains!' they screeched. 'Pull harder!' and they heaved with all their might. Suddenly the old wires came loose, and the curtains crashed to the floor.

" 'Look!' I shrieked.

"There crouched the strangers for all to see, pounding the floor with chains and bellowing at the top of their lungs. The two made a dash for the side door, but they weren't fast enough. The audience wrestled them to the floor, took back every nickel that had been collected, and sent the imposters down Vinegar Lane.

"Then folks began to thank *me* for exposing the hoax. I tried to explain, but no one listened. Finally I just said, 'My pleasure,' over and over, smiling and nodding while my cousins untied my boots from the curtain fringes. At last everyone began to drift off home.

"'Come on, Nellie, let's go,' said my cousins. But they didn't pull on my arms. They didn't hiss at me. And they didn't say another word about being bored, not then or ever."

Nellie Mouse laid down her needle.

"There, Freddie," she said, "my embroidery and my tale are done."

Papa held up Freddie's skis in the firelight. "Look," he said. "All fixed."

"And my paw feels much better," said Freddie. "Those tales helped a lot. I'm sure I can ski again tomorrow."

"I'll come with you," Henry said.

"Me, too," said George and Ella.

Nellie Mouse stifled a yawn and bowed toward Mama and Papa Fox. "I must say good night."

Grammer and Granky began to put on their scarves. "Happy skiing tomorrow, Freddie."

"I, too, must bid you farewell," said Bert Blue Jay.

Then Grammer and Granky went out the front door, Nellie Mouse disappeared into her home in the pantry, and Bert Blue Jay raised his wing in salute before flying off through the window that Papa Fox opened for him.

"It was a lovely winter's eve," said Mama.

"It was indeed," said Papa.

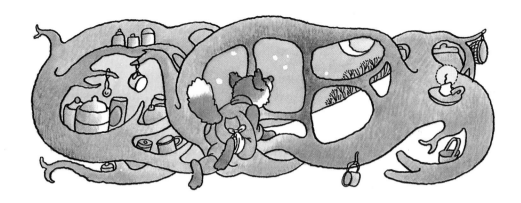

# GOOD NIGHT

FREDDIE RAN to the window to look out at the winter night. The windows of Vinegar Lane were dark now. Bare trees marched up over snow-covered hills, row after row. Overhead, the pale moon floated high.

Finally, Freddie let Mama carry him to the warm bench by the fire, where he held his paws up so the nightshirt could slip over his head. He followed Ella and George and Henry down the cold passageway to the bedchamber.

Ella set the candle on the nightstand, and they all climbed quickly into their beds. They shivered, and waited to get warm under their quilts. Mama came to tuck them in. As she lifted

the candle from the nightstand, shadows jumped crazily all over the room.

"Good night," said Mama, as she kissed them. "Sleep tight."

"Good night," said the older children, one by one.

"Good night," said Freddie, last of all.

He watched Mama's big black shape with its halo of candle-light go away down the hall and disappear around the corner. The room was dark.

Freddie snuggled into his quilt. His paw felt warm and comfortable now. He turned his head on his pillow, to watch the moon through the window, until finally his eyes shut and he fell asleep.